For my sister Kathleen Clark   MM
For Mum and Dad   DM

Text © 1991 Maryann Macdonald
Illustrations © 1991 Dave McTaggart

First published 1991 by ABC, All Books for Children
a division of The All Children's Company Ltd
10 Museum Street, London WC1A 1JS

Printed and bound in Hong Kong by Imago Services (H.K.) Ltd.

British Library Cataloguing in Publication Data
Macdonald, Maryann
Ben at the beach.
I. Title II. McTaggart, Dave
823.914 [J]

ISBN 1-85406-091-0

Ben at the Beach

By Maryann Macdonald

Illustrated by Dave McTaggart

ABC
London

Grandma was taking Ben and Charlotte to the beach.

Ben had a new fishing rod. "I am going to catch a big, big fish!" he said.

Charlotte had a bucket and a shovel. "Me dig," she said. "Dig big."

At last they got to the beach.

"May I go fishing now, Grandma?" Ben asked.

"All right, Ben," said Grandma.

So Ben took his fishing rod and went off to the dock.

"Sorry," the man said. "No children allowed."

Ben walked slowly back to the beach.

He tried to cast his line into the deep water where big fish live. But his line was too short.

He tried to catch little fish in the shallow water. But the little fish would not bite.

"Ben," called Grandma. "Come and play with Charlotte now!"

Ben sighed. "Oh, well," he thought. He could take Charlotte wading in the cool water.

But Charlotte did not like the water.
She would not go in.

"Monsters!" she yelled when waves whooshed
up. She grabbed Ben and held on tight.

"Nice water," said Ben. He splashed gently.
"Bad water!" yelled Charlotte. She started to cry.

"Don't cry," said Ben. He got Charlotte's bucket
and spade. "Dig?" he asked. "Dig big?"
Charlotte nodded.
So Ben dug a big hole with Charlotte.

They made holes all around it.

They put seashells and stones on the walls.

Last of all, Ben dug a moat.

"Now," he said to Charlotte, "comes the best part!"

He took her bucket and waded into the shallow
water. He filled it with water and tiny fish.

Then he poured the
water into the moat.

Charlotte saw the fish shining in the sunlight. "Pretty!" she said. "More!"
"Your turn," said Ben.

He took Charlotte's hand. Charlotte held
Ben's hand tightly. She waded with him
slowly into the shallow water.
She took the bucket.
She filled it with water and tiny fish.

She emptied it into the moat.
Then she smiled proudly at Ben.

"Congratulations!" said a man. "You win
first prize in the sandcastle contest."

First prize was a boat. Grandma helped them blow it up. Then they all got in. Grandma paddled.

Charlotte watched out for sea monsters.

And Ben caught a big fish in the deep water.

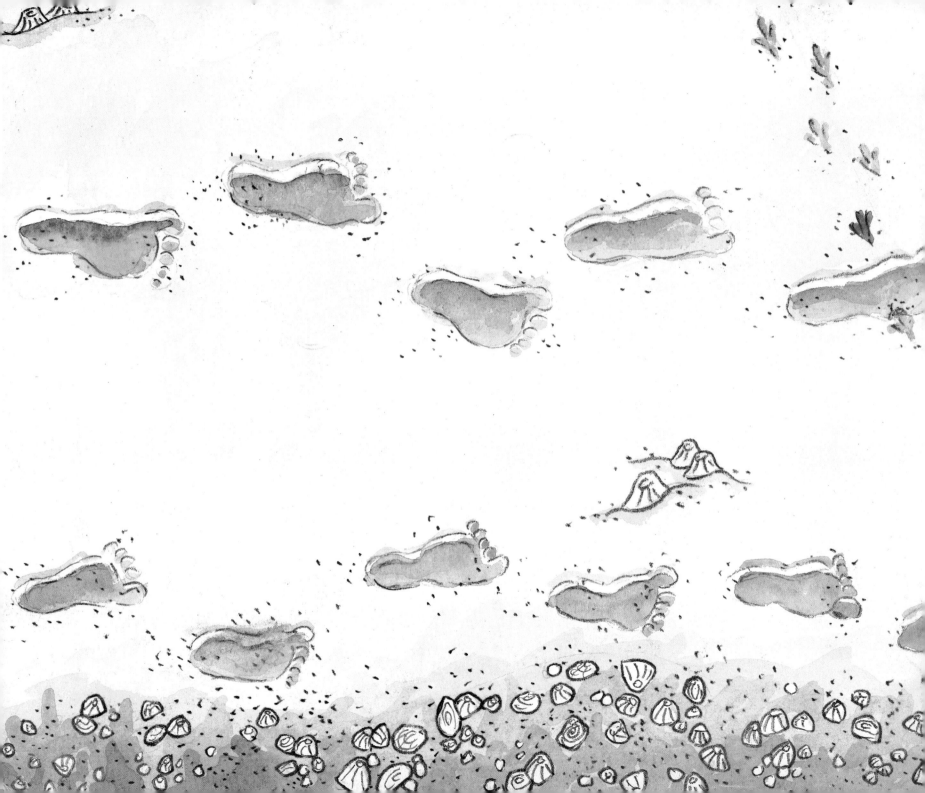